Hi! I'm Max.

What's your name?

My mom and dad are taking me to the zoo today.

There's so much to learn there, and it'll be lots of fun!

Do you want to come along?

There's the ticket booth!
How many tickets do we need to buy?
One for my mom, one for my dad, one for me, and one for you - that makes four!

Ooh! We can also get a map to guide us through the zoo!
I wonder which animal we'll see first. What do you think it will be?

Wow! The flamingos are first!
My mom told me their feathers are pink
because they eat lots of shrimp.
Isn't that strange?

Can you see the flamingo with her head in the water?
She must be using her long neck to search for food right now!

Some of them are standing on only one leg!
Can you stand on one leg like a flamingo? Let's try together!

Whoa! Here are the zebras!

Do you see how they
don't look exactly alike?
That's because every zebra
has a unique pattern
of black and white stripes.

Also, did you know that
zebras can run really fast?
They can even outrun a lion!
I think that's amazing!
How fast can you run?

There are the giraffes -
the tallest animals in the world!
Their long necks help them reach leaves
from the tops of very tall trees.

Oh! Look at the giraffe being fed by that little girl.
Can you see his super dark tongue? It's nearly black!
That dark color protects it from getting a sunburn.

Yay! Here are my favorite animals - the elephants!

Those big white teeth are called tusks.
And look at their long trunks! Elephants use their trunks to do lots of things,
like breathe, smell, and pick up food.
They can even use them to squirt water into their mouths!

Ooh! The baby elephant is using
her trunk to hold her mom's tail,
kind of like how I hold my mom's hand!

If you had a trunk like an elephant,
what would you do with it?

Wow! The lions!
They are so strong
and powerful.

That must be the dad on the top of the rocks.
Do you see the hair around his face? That's called a mane.

The mom is sleeping next to her baby cub.
He doesn't look very tired, though. It looks like he wants to play!

And here's another big cat -
the tiger!

There's water in his enclosure
because he actually likes to swim!
He prefers being alone, though,
so he gets this whole area to himself.

I really love his stripes,
and orange is my favorite color.
What's your favorite color?

Here is the rhinoceros!
He roams on land and likes to munch on grass.
And look! The hippopotamus is next to him!

I used to get these two animals mixed up,
but my dad helped me remember:
"rhino" means nose, so the one with
the horn on his nose is the rhinoceros!

The hippopotamus
likes to eat grass, too, but see -
he has a huge mouth and giant teeth!

He really loves spending time in the water because it keeps him cool.
I love playing in the water like a hippo! Do you?

Whoa! Gorillas!

Do you see the
ones with silver backs?
Those are the dads.
They are humongous!

And look at all the others -
there are moms, kids, and babies.

How many gorillas can you see? Let's count them together:
1, 2, 3, 4, 5, 6, 7, 8...9!

Gorillas are part of the ape family,
and their arms are longer than their legs.
They walk on their knuckles and feet!

Can you walk like a gorilla?
Let's try it out!

We've found the monkeys!

They are primates like the gorillas, but see - they are much smaller, and they have tails.

Monkeys use their tails
to swing from tree to tree.
They also use them for balance!

Did you know they really like to eat bananas? I do, too! What's your favorite fruit?

Here are the giant pandas!
This panda mom has twin panda babies.
(That means she had two babies at the same time.)

Do you want to hear my panda song?
Sing along with me!

Now we've reached
the koalas and kangaroos!

These animals are
called marsupials
because the moms
have pouches to
hold their babies.

Look! You can see
two baby kangaroos
peeking out!

Oh, and do you see how all the koalas are sleeping?
That's because they're mostly nocturnal, and they love to sleep during the day.

The kangaroos are wide awake, though!
Did you know that kangaroos don't really walk or run? They just like to hop!
Can you hop like a kangaroo? Let's hop to our last stop!

Here we are!
It's the butterfly garden!

Look at all the different colors and patterns
on their wings. They are so beautiful!

Do you see how they're flying from flower to flower?
They're drinking sweet nectar from each one.

Did you know that
butterflies actually
start out as
caterpillars?

They go through
metamorphosis
and completely
change their bodies!

There's the zoo train!
Have you ever
ridden on a train?

Let's hop on for a ride!

We can talk about
all the new things
we learned today!

Why is a giraffe's tongue so dark?

What kinds of things can an elephant do with its trunk?

Can you remember what a baby lion is called?

Which animal has a horn on its nose – the rhino or the hippo?

Do you know what pandas like to eat?

What are the animals called that carry their babies in a pouch?

Aaaand... what was your favorite animal that you saw today?

Ooh! I almost forgot to tell you a joke I just heard -
What kind of key opens a banana?

A mon-key!! Hahahahahahaha!

Thank you for coming to the zoo with me! I had so much fun learning with you!
Maaaaybe, just maybe, we can go to a farm next time.
See you soon!

"Do You Want to Come to the Zoo With Me?"

By: Ashley Tadayeski, aka "Max & Leo's Mom"
Illustrations by: Laia Design Lab

Hardcover ISBN: 978-1-7358214-0-5
Paperback ISBN: 978-1-7358214-1-2

Library of Congress Control Number: 2020924417

FIRST EDITION

Printed by Ingram Spark
in the United States of America.

www.maxandleobooks.com
 @maxandleobooks

CPSIA information can be obtained
at www.ICGtesting.com
Printed in the USA
LVHW072019210421
685034LV00024B/19